ANWAR'S STORY

ANWAR'S STORY

A Fable Based On
The Alchemist by Paulo Coelho

Karen Williams

Copyright © 2020 Karen Williams

ISBN: 978-0-244-24743-0

All rights reserved, including the right to reproduce this book, or portions thereof in any form. No part of this text may be reproduced, transmitted, downloaded, decompiled, reverse engineered, or stored, in any form or introduced into any information storage and retrieval system, in any form or by any means, whether electronic or mechanical without the express written permission of the author.

Cover illustration courtesy of Shutterstock.com
Interior illustration courtesy of Shutterstock.com

DEDICATION

To
Daddy and Mama.
Thank-you for everything.

To
Paulo Coelho.
Thank-you for daring to dream.

And to
Mohammed Bendaanane.
Thank-you for sharing your story.

CONTENTS

AUTHOR'S NOTE

PART I
THE BEGINNING

Memories
The Terror

PART II
THE RECKONING

Despair
The Dream

PART III
REDEMPTION

The Darkness Before The Dawn
Treasure
The Return

FINAL NOTE

About the Author

TRUTH IS STRANGER THAN FICTION

AND

IGNORANCE IS NOT ALWAYS BLISS.

There are two ways to be fooled.

One is to believe

WHAT ISN'T TRUE;

the other is to refuse to believe

WHAT IS TRUE.

SOREN KIERKEGAARD

AUTHOR'S NOTE

Dear Friend,

Anwar's Story is a fable I have written, some of it channeled from an invisible spiritual realm, which tells the fictional story of the *other hero* in the iconic, bestselling book The Alchemist by Paulo Coelho.

"What other hero?" I hear you ask. For millions of readers of The Alchemist the book is simply a fable about a young Andalusian shepherd boy called Santiago who dreams of finding treasure near the pyramids of Egypt, and who abandons everything in his life in pursuit of that dream. After many challenges, and life lessons, he then finally finds his treasure in a truly unexpected and paradoxical way. Well, dear friend, my fable will reveal to you that this is not actually the whole story.

In 1995, when I had never heard of Paulo Coelho or his famous allegory, I was living on a hill in the Andalusian countryside in southern Spain. At the beginning of that year I embarked on a spiritual quest to find my soul as a result of experiencing a very deep dream. My quest began in more or less exactly the same way as it had for Santiago because the dream came to me one night after returning from visiting an old, abandoned ruin high on a hill near my parents' house.

That life-changing dream took me to Tarifa and Tangiers, just as Santiago's dream had in The Alchemist and then, like Santiago, I found myself leaving Tangiers and embarking on a journey through a desert. In the shepherd's case it was the Sahara desert, however in mine it was a metaphorical desert in England.

After nine months in my personal 'wilderness' I eventually arrived at my destination – a land of pyramids. Although these pyramids were not the pyramids of Egypt as they were for Paulo's shepherd boy, they were *symbolically equivalent* to the Egyptian pyramids in The Alchemist. There I endured a 'beating' in much the same way as Santiago had at the end of his own journey and then, just like Santiago, I was finally given my true treasure by the man who 'beat' me.

When I returned to Andalusia I was sent a copy of The Alchemist by some Spanish friends, and on reading it for the very first time in my life, was surprised and astonished to discover some of these peculiar 'coincidences' between myself and the so-called 'fictional' hero of Paulo Coelho's tale. However, being still a novice in my own spiritual quest, it was only four years later that the universe revealed to me why this was so.

As I stood on a hill in April 2000, looking at the ruin which I had visited before having my powerful dream, I suddenly experienced a cosmic flash of insight and was shown that I was in fact the real-life Santiago of Paulo's fable, and that his book was not completely a work of fiction.

***

The truth is that Paulo had unconsciously channeled his story from an invisible spiritual realm, and in so doing had inadvertently predicted the future. That future then happened to me in real life seven years after the publication of The Alchemist in 1988. This is an example of:

LIFE IMITATING ART.

In 2014, in an interview with Oprah Winfrey in his home in Geneva, Paulo posed Oprah the following question:

> "But, Oprah, you want to know, did I write The Alchemist? I'm not sure. I'm sure that I was a good instrument."

Paulo was alluding to the truth with his question and answer to Oprah, but never went so far as to use the word 'channeled.'

Back in the year 2000, when I was given the unexpected insight that I was Santiago in Paulo's book, this spurred me on to continue with my quest for the light of my soul, and like the shepherd boy I abandoned and risked everything in my life in order to find that inner treasure. In the process the journey allowed me to make two completely 'accidental' discoveries of two extraordinary truths.

The first of those truths is that The Alchemist is a classical example of Joseph Campbell's Hero's Journey, and the second is that the fable contains a hidden, spiritual archetype:

the archetype of Mankind's journey in search of redemption.

When I uncovered that archetype in the fable, it became obvious to me that this same archetype was at the heart of the original story from the Arabian Nights on which Paulo had based The Alchemist, and so both stories had never just been about one hero and his personal adventures.

No, there were actually two heroes!

Santiago was not the only protagonist of The Alchemist. His long journey and final discovery of his treasure had only been made possible because he had encountered the *other hero* within this archetype.

***

On making my second discovery, a huge horizon of new understanding opened up before me on my quest, and it became clear to me that those two heroes in Paulo's fable were actually personifications or symbols of the two halves of the human soul. Yes, dear friend, quite unconsciously each half of the soul, physically incarnated by Santiago and the leader of the refugees, goes in search of its other half.

Their journeys into the outside world are the only way in which both of these heroes can meet, and in so doing find their respective treasures.

When Santiago is beaten by the 'other half' of his soul at the end of his journey it is because he encounters a physical personification of that part of his soul which is his ego; an ego consumed with an obsessive desire to find treasure for himself, and only for himself. And so, the alchemical heart of The Alchemist is that it is only when the shepherd boy has had an encounter with his own inner darkness that the light of his soul – his treasure – can be revealed to him.

But, equally, the leader of the refugees also encounters his own darkness by meeting Santiago, and through that encounter also finally finds his personal treasure.

Paulo Coelho was completely unaware of the *other hero* hidden inside his fable, and so never addressed the fate of Santiago's 'other half'. But as you will discover within these pages, my friend, there truly is another story to be told; the story of this other man.

***

After 23 years on a spiritual odyssey, I finally brought out the story of my quest in my book TREASURE: NEW EDITION III, and in it I placed a short channeled account of how the leader of the refugees received his own treasure from Santiago at the very end of Paulo's fable.

I contacted Paulo Coelho many times as I wrote my book to share with him the fact that there were actually two heroes and not just one in his book. But unfortunately, by the time I had managed to 'pop out' from seemingly nowhere to tell him all of this, The Alchemist had already become a worldwide bestseller and so I don't think Paulo was quite able to digest or believe any of what I had to say.

Although, as I have just said, I told a small part of the leader of the refugees' story in TREASURE, in the months that followed, after bringing out my book in 2019, I felt drawn to delving into the possible life of this *other hero* of Paulo's tale. Who was this invisible man, and what was his story? That delving took the form of many sleepless nights during which my imagination journeyed into his psyche and what had led him to his fateful meeting with Santiago.

Then, about ten days ago dear friend, to my utter surprise I got up one night, switched on my computer and began to write this fable you have before you. I allowed it to flow out of me – and flow it did. That is always a sign to any writer that what they are typing onto the page is uniquely important, possibly in some way channeled from another realm, and most definitely NEEDS to be told.

In TREASURE I had called this 'invisible man' Anwar because in Arabic Anwar means light. And this of course is what these two protagonists of Paulo's fable so desperately wanted to find, even if only subconsciously – the light of their souls hidden in their other halves.

Santiago's story and Anwar's story taken together answer many readers' questions which have been metaphorically left 'hanging in the air' for over three decades since Paulo first published The Alchemist. And by answering those questions, I have finally been able to give you, and all the readers of Paulo's fable, the missing piece which makes this iconic and beloved story whole.

***

I hope you enjoy my creation of Anwar's life and spirit, and my imagining of this untold half of Paulo's fable. Paulo was right when he said to Oprah Winfrey in 2014 that he had been a 'good instrument' when writing his book, but unknown to him he *was not the only one!*

The universe exhibits an uncanny precision in its workings, and will do everything it can to make the truth known, using whatever and whoever in order to accomplish that goal.

However, more often than not, it may decide to take an extremely long time to do so – at least it may seem that way from our very limited human perspective.

And so it has taken more than thirty years to reveal The Alchemist's *other hero's* story through its 'other instrument' – namely me! But, 'better late than never' as the saying goes. The result of those 'workings' is here before you my friend. I sincerely wish you an interesting and illuminating read.

England: November 22nd 2019

PART I
THE BEGINNING

MEMORIES

THE music was loud and intoxicating, and seemed to be coming from everywhere around them. Beautiful women in amazing dresses the colours of rainbows and exotic birds twirled around in the main square. With them danced men wearing elegant trousers, black boots, tailored waistcoats and dashing hats. Other men on horseback watched from the sidelines, occasionally making their horses trot on the spot in time to the music.

Wine flowed and children in similar colourful clothes ran about laughing and shouting as they dove in and out between the large groups of adults. Delicious smells of barbecued meat filled the air and Anwar knew only too well that he was once again in his own personal heaven.

This was the Fair in Ronda which his father and mother brought him to each year at the end of their annual summer stay in Andalusia. These were the last bittersweet few days for the family before they returned to their home in Tangiers in Morocco. Life there was not as carefree for them as it was here.

***

Anwar's father was Egyptian, and his mother half French and half Egyptian. They were an odd couple. Anwar knew their story inside out because he had been told it over and over again by his mother.

She had met his father in Cairo at a local market when they had both been teenagers. Omar was probably the handsomest young man his mother had ever seen, and he seemed to notice her every time she went to the market for fruit, vegetables and meat. After a few encounters they had begun to talk, and something began to grow between them. Celeste knew that Omar was special and unlike all the other boys she had met. To begin with he spoke excellent French, and he also liked to share his poems with her.

His eyes were deep, dark, velvety pools, but touched with sadness, and in them she saw that he sensed her own sadness. Somehow, for very different reasons, both of these young people could not connect with the world in which they lived. Celeste felt cursed by her 'otherness' – she was neither French nor Egyptian – and Omar seemed to be different too.

As well as his poems, occasionally Omar would bring a record of songs to the market sung by his favourite singer Umm Kulthum. "This is Egyptian poetry sung by the best singer in the Arab world Celeste." he would tell her. "Take it home and listen." Celeste dutifully listened to the songs on Omar's records and knew in her heart that they were love letters to her from this young man who made her pulse race and filled her thoughts each night as she lay awake dreaming of another life.

One day they both managed to escape the market for a few hours to spend some time alone. As they talked, Celeste could see that Omar was not his usual bright self; he seemed troubled and anxious in a way he had never been before.

"I want to see the world," Omar confessed to her, "this is not where I belong. I love my parents, and I know they love me, but I can't be what they want me to be, and I can't face spending the rest of my life in the market when my parents have gone. I want to be a great poet and change people's lives."

Celeste listened intently to Omar's words, sensing that his heart was actually confessing something else to her – his deep, undying love for her. Suddenly, she found herself impulsively plucking up some kind of courage from an unknown place within herself as she nervously reached out for Omar's hand. As she touched it, she felt strange, unexpected words tumble from her mouth. "Where shall we go Omar? Where shall we go?"

Six months later, these two young souls had made their plans. They would elope, leave Cairo and take the camel train west. They had saved enough money for the journey, and they would try to reach Morocco. Morocco was close to Europe, and that was where Celeste had been born – in Marseille she had told Omar with uncontainable pride! They had looked at maps and Tangiers was the logical destination for them.

They could live and work there for a while to save more money and then make the short sea journey across the Strait of Gibraltar to Spain – the gateway to Europe and their new lives. And so, that is exactly what Anwar's parents did. With their youthful love and dreams, Omar and Celeste boarded the camel train to their future.

***

They had been wise enough to take the precaution of seeming as if they were married. Celeste assumed her arabic second name of Farah, constantly referred to Omar as her husband and did not speak French throughout the whole journey to Morocco. Omar meanwhile busied himself reading Arabic poetry and imitating the behaviour of the rest of the men who they were travelling with.

The other women teased Celeste about babies, and what a handsome man she had married. No one knew the truth about this strange, young couple who said they were on their way to visit their family in Tangiers. Finally, at the end of their journey Omar and Celeste found a night's lodgings with one of the families whom they had befriended on the camel train, and then in the morning they said their farewells and boarded an ancient-looking bus to Tangiers.

"A year later you were born Anwar" his mother used to tell him, and that it seemed was also when his parents' dreams of Europe had come to an abrupt end. His arrival had meant that his father had needed to find enough work to sustain them all, and so the Hassan family's life became Omar's workshop in Tangiers and his mother's job as a cook to a local French family. They never talked about travelling to Marseille again.

But, despite this change in their circumstances, for Anwar's parents life could never be just as it was for their neighbours in Tangiers. His father would not allow their humble life to restrict him and his family in any way. They were poor, and France had become beyond their reach, but Omar continued to write his poems, and dream of a bigger, wider world than the one in which they lived.

***

Each summer from the middle of August until the middle of September Anwar and his parents would take the small ferry boat from Tangiers to the small port of Tarifa in Spain to spend four weeks in Andalusia. Omar knew that his skills as a craftsman in wood were highly sought after in Andalusia, and his exotic Moroccan pieces were always a great success amongst the inhabitants of the small towns along the Mediterranean coast.

The family had begun these trips to Spain when Anwar was only three years old, and by the time he was six he had already mastered enough Spanish to be able to play with the local children in Tarifa.

Every year, at the end of their four week stay, the great treat was to journey inland to the small historic town of Ronda and spend three days at the Fair. This particular year was a special one for Anwar. He had just turned eight years old, and his father had told him that he would now be showing him how to carve wood in the workshop after school, and also letting him sell pieces in the market on their return to Tangiers.

This made their final days in Ronda less sad for Anwar and at the end of their visit, as they took the bus back down the mountain towards Tarifa on the coast, his thoughts were filled with the idea of being able to spend more time with his father, learning from him, and even making some money of his own. However, only nine short months after those dreams, everything in Anwar's life had changed. His father was gone.

Anwar and his mother stood on the quayside of the harbour in Tangiers and watched the flowers they had brought floating on the surface of the water. Another woman and her children stood beside them. This was Ahmed's wife and family. Ahmed had been Omar's fishing companion. On their days off the two men had enjoyed taking Ahmed's little boat out into the Strait of Gibraltar to fish.

Night time was always the best time for this. Both men knew that they would be tired the next day, but the fishing in the dark always landed them their biggest catches, and gave them that extra money they needed for their families. However, now the two men were dead.

Three days earlier a storm had begun to gather in the early evening and Celeste had begged her husband not to fish that night. But Omar had assured his wife that the storm would stay inland and never reach the sea.

"I've been out in much worse Celeste," Omar told her, hoping to distract his beloved from her fears, "and besides, you know that nothing bad ever happens to us. Sometimes Ahmed and I have the best trips when we have to fight the sea a little. That's when we catch the most fish!"

Celeste had not been convinced by Omar's words, and had spent the whole night awake awaiting his usual return in the early hours of the morning. Nevertheless, when the dawn light had finally arrived through the windows of their small house, her husband was nowhere to be seen. Celeste had left the house and rushed down to the port to see if he was still there. And then that was when she had seen the faces of the fishermen as she had approached the quay – faces of shock and death.

Anwar had awoken in the house a few hours later to find it empty, and he too had made his way to the port in search of his mother. He had found her there, buried in her tears, wailing like an animal, and repeating the name of her husband over and over again. In that moment, even though his young mind couldn't quite grasp what had happened, Anwar's heart had died with his father.

***

The days after that morning turned into a blur of shock. Anwar's mother forced her son to go to school in the mornings, but on his return they would sit in the kitchen and cry together, unable to speak or even enter the workshop where Omar had spent each afternoon with his son. A month passed in this way, and then one afternoon Celeste turned to Anwar and told him that they were leaving Tangiers for good.

"We have no money Anwar. I have to sell what your father has made, and then we will return to my parents in Egypt. We cannot stay here."

That return journey for mother and son was a journey like

no other. It was an encounter with a black, endless hole. All their memories of Omar were still in Tangiers and Andalusia. There had been no body to bury, and his absence seemed to have made time stand still and the world around them look like some strange place devoid of all meaning. The only thing they knew for certain was that they had each other, and it was only when they sat together that Omar returned to them; as young, vibrant and loving as he had been on the night he had left the house to fish with his friend Ahmed.

Eventually after many, long weeks the caravan reached the outskirts of Cairo, and the smell of the city greeted them well before they reached its bustling centre. Everything about the place overwhelmed Anwar's senses. The frenzy of activity was frightening to this young boy; he had never seen so many people, cars, carts, trucks and dirt. His mother had been away from her family for ten long years, and although she knew where they lived, she had no idea how she and her son would be received by them.

After about a half-hour walk through alleyways and streets Anwar and his mother eventually arrived at a large pink house. It was clearly the largest house in the street, and owned by rather wealthy people. "We have arrived, my son." his mother announced quietly.

"Where?" said Anwar in a state of bewilderment.

"This is where I grew up Anwar. This is your grandfather and grandmother's house."

***

His mother moved forward as she held his hand, and rang a bell on the side of a large wooden door. About fifteen seconds later the door swung open and a man who appeared to be a servant looked down on them. He seemed a little taken aback and then somewhat puzzled to see a young woman and boy in front of him. He stared long and hard at Anwar's mother, and then his eyes appeared to suddenly jump out of their sockets.

"Mademoiselle Celeste! Is it you?" he cried, almost falling off his feet in a state of utter disbelief.

Anwar's mother replied that it was she, and then called the man by a strange name. He bowed in respect to her, and she slowly moved through the open door, still holding Anwar's hand. They entered a dimly lit corridor and that was the moment when Anwar remembered that his life had changed forever.

THE TERROR

HIS uncle beat him again and again with his stick. Anwar had sold very little in the market that day and the rent was due.

"You are scum, Anwar, scum." his uncle raged. "You killed your mother. Because of you she stayed with that man whose name I will never speak for as long as I live. You and he ruined her life, and killed her, and this family will never forget that."

Anwar knew that this was a lie, but with each blow that his uncle gave him, it felt more and more like the truth. In fact, after so many years of this terror, Anwar had begun to lose all grip on what was or wasn't real in his life.

Within a year of their return to Cairo, when Anwar was still only nine years old, his mother had caught a cold and died. Anwar had seen his mother become weaker and weaker with every passing month they had spent with his grandparents and he had understood that it had never been the cold which had taken her life, but her broken heart. She had never stopped talking about his father, and on her last day she had given him a poem Omar had written to her when Anwar had been born.

"We called you Anwar because it means light, my darling." she had whispered to him, her voice now weak from illness. "You were our light. You were the fruit of our love, so never forget that my son."

She had caressed his face gently with her cold hands, and those had been her last words to him. A week later Anwar's uncle had seen him reading the poem and had torn it out of his hands and burned it. With that cruel act, Anwars' living hell on Earth had begun.

***

After the death of his mother, Anwar's uncle Mazir had told his grandparents that they were far too old to look after him and that he would take care of the boy. Anwar had found himself virtually kidnapped by his uncle and taken to live alone with this sadistic man in his house on the other side of Cairo.

Year in and year out life was the agony that Mazir dished out to his nephew. Anwar's uncle had a market stall in the neighbourhood where they lived and at which he sold hookah pipes. He was a lazy man, and also an addict. He lived as far away from his family as he could so that no one would discover his addiction to hashish. By the time Anwar was eleven years old he was running his uncle's stall single-handedly whilst Mazir stayed at home smoking all day long.

Most of the men at the market were nothing more than petty thieves and hustlers. One of them constantly supplied Mazir with his hashish in exchange for Anwar giving him twenty percent of their profits. Other children of Anwar's age were still at school, but Anwar's life was now the hours he spent in the market and the dark nights of watching his uncle lying on his couch, completely out of his senses from huge overdoses of his preferred drug.

Having once been a loving and trusting boy, as each year passed Anwar found himself becoming an angry and vicious adolescent. He learned quickly from the men in the market how to fool his clients, and also how to make a little extra money by exchanging stolen goods. His grandparents had died two years after he had gone to live with his uncle, and with this news the very last glimmer of any hope for his life had been erased from his heart forever.

Five years later when Anwar was sixteen, and finally growing into a young man, all he wanted to do was kill Mazir. He would lie awake each night imagining how he would do it. He could feel the rope in his hands, and could see himself tying the rope around his uncle's neck as he slept. Doped up as he always was, Mazir would never feel anything, and so Anwar could strangle him and then throw his body down the dry well inside the kitchen courtyard.

He knew that this fantasy of his was terribly wrong, but his suffering at the hands of this man was so intense that he felt such a wrong would be utterly excusable. After the killing, he would hide out in the desert for a few weeks and then, when it was safe, he would return to the city, join the camel train, and leave Egypt for good.

He imagined himself returning to Tangiers where he had been a boy. Then he would take the boat across the Strait of Gibraltar and go back to Ronda, marry one of the pretty Andalusian girls he had seen spinning around in those amazing dresses at the Fair so many years ago, and he would never have to remember how his mother had died of a broken heart.

But, each morning when the light filtered into the filth of the house he shared with his uncle, and his eyelids unglued themselves, his rage and hatred left him and were replaced by hunger and the need to make money at the market. Another day had passed when Anwar had not been able to kill his uncle and find his freedom.

***

One morning in the middle of winter, when Anwar was already nineteen years old, and now a fully-grown adult, he woke up as usual for his daily grind when he noticed something different. His uncle was not in his bed. Anwar went into the kitchen to see if some kind of miracle had occurred and his uncle had woken up before him and had begun to prepare their breakfast. But, no, the kitchen was empty.

He moved into the small living space which reeked with the stench of hashish, and saw that this room was empty too. As he was about to enter his uncle's bedroom, he saw that the front door of the house was open. He walked over to it and peered outside. That was when he nearly jumped out of his own skin. His uncle lay motionless on the ground, and his body was blue. He was dead.

Anwar's first thought was to drag his uncle's body back into the house and call the police to inform them of the death, but the adrenalin he felt coursing through his body at that very instant could not be controlled. Instead he started to run away as fast as his legs would carry him from what had been his home for so many terrible and desperate years.

He was tired but he ran like a madman possessed. He ran and ran until after about twenty minutes he found himself out in the desert staring at the Giza Pyramids in the distance. He looked around him and saw that there was no one about. The sun had barely risen above the horizon and the air was still bitterly cold. Suddenly his brain seemed to grind to a halt, and he felt himself stop breathing. And then everything around him went black.

When he regained consciousness, and finally opened his eyes, he realised that he was lying in a bed in some kind of infirmary. A nurse hovered around another bed and another patient. Slowly he turned his head to one side and saw an old man lying in the bed next to him. He looked like one of the city's beggars, or a tramp, and the smell emanating from his body was horrendous.

Anwar felt himself start to gag and retch and within seconds he had vomited an acid bile from his stomach all over the sheet covering his neck and chest. The nurse spotted the drama and quickly ran over to him.

"Please, please, I can't stand the smell," Anwar begged the nurse, "move me, please."

The nurse rushed up to a tall, thin man in a long white coat who looked to be a doctor. They chatted for a few brief moments and then the doctor approached Anwar's bed and told him to go to a room at the end of the ward. Once in the room, the doctor began to take Anwar's pulse and listen to his heart and lungs through his stethoscope.

"You are fine, young man," he said, "you just blacked out, and some camel drivers found you and brought you here. We are not a proper hospital, but a charity, and so we can't keep you here. You can go home now." and with those words the doctor turned around and left.

***

"You can go home now." Anwar repeated the words to himself over and over again. *BUT HE HAD NO HOME!!!* That was what he wanted to scream at the doctor at the top of his voice! His uncle was dead and now he had no family.

He felt bitterness and anger return to him, and a fiery rage erupt inside his body. He hated Cairo – absolutely hated the city. It had taken his mother, given him the hell he had lived through with his uncle, and he knew that he had never belonged here in the first place. Anwar belonged to where he had lived with his father and mother.

Now suddenly, from out of nowhere, he could not stop thinking about his father whom he had lost all those years ago. During the ten years he had spent with his uncle he had refused to allow himself to remember the past. The pain of his young life with this man had been so extreme that to remember what he had lost would surely have destroyed him. But now, something outside of himself had taken him over.

He could see his father's face so clearly. His smile, his beard. The man who had taught Anwar how to make so many wonderful things with wood, and who had told him so often how much he loved him. His father who had taken his mother and himself to Spain, to Ronda, to Tarifa and to all the other magical places he had loved as a child.

The rage which he had felt starting to course through his body began to consume him like a wildfire. Anwar knew that he had to get out of the city for his own sanity; at that moment madness felt very close.

Then, without warning, his father's image disappeared and instead he saw the face of a woman appear in his mind's eye. It was Amira the fortune teller. He remembered a conversation he had once had with her when she had worked in the market with him and the other men. One day she had taken Anwar to her house, and had read his palm. She had told him that his uncle was a sick man and would die soon, but he hadn't believed her.

Now, his uncle really was dead, just as Amira had predicted, and so his next thought was that maybe he should try to find this woman with the special gift, and ask her what he should do next.

***

A few hours later Anwar was sitting on the Persian carpet in Amira's house waiting for her to place her special oil on his palm and tell him his future. Amira squatted down beside Anwar and performed her ritual. Then she shut her eyes tightly and began to hum. A few seconds later she opened them and looked deep into Anwar's eyes.

"You are in great danger my boy," she said. "Cairo will kill you, or you will kill Cairo. You must leave the city at once."

"I know," said Anwar in a state of frenzy, "I know, but where can I go?"

Amira paused and shut her eyes again. "The desert my son, you must go into the desert. There you will meet some men. They are refugees from the clan wars. You will join them, and then become their leader. They will be your family. You will find yourself with them."

Anwar felt such total desperation in his heart that he could do nothing else but believe this woman.

"Where will they be Amira? I can't just walk out into the desert. You must tell me more."

Amira opened her eyes. "They will be at the pyramids of Giza. You don't have to recognise them; they will recognise you. A hawk will circle around your head in the sky above you and that will be their sign. Now, go. I have told you your future – there is nothing more to say."

Without another word Amira got up and walked to the door. She opened it and stared out into the street. It seemed as though she was in some kind of trance. Anwar raised himself and walked towards the door. He looked at her briefly and saw a bewitching smile flicker across her face.

"It is written, my son, it is written. Allah knows everything. Now go."

Anwar stepped into the street and the door slammed shut behind him.

PART II
THE RECKONING

DESPAIR

TEN years in the desert had brought Anwar back to his feelings of despair and pain. The last battle he had fought with his men in the desert had been a defining moment for him. It had tipped him over his personal edge, and now he knew that he simply couldn't go on.

Just as Amira had told him all those years ago, when he had been nineteen years old, he had found the men near the Giza Pyramids and Allah had given him a 'family'.

At first the life with these men had been everything he could possibly have dreamed of. After a few months with them he had forgotten about his cruel uncle and the decade of pain he had endured with him. He had even forgotten about his mother and father. The life he had shared with these men was the stuff of legends. There had been the battles in the desert, the camaraderie between his new 'brothers', the magic of the desert itself, stories shared, deep bonds forged through danger faced together, and always, yes, always the promise of another adventure.

Of course it was true that it had not all been good. He had seen friends die, and now he remembered his dearest friend, Hamza. His death had been unbearable for Anwar. They had been so close, and for weeks after his loss Anwar had been unable to find any meaning in the life he had chosen. But his comrades had supported him through it all, and slowly the excitement had returned.

Then, soon after Hamza's death, Anwar had been promoted to second-in-command of the clan, and finally three years later he had found himself the 'leader of the pack'.

Now, as he stood in the alleyway in front of Amira's house

ten years later, a thought suddenly struck him. *Had he really chosen the life he had been living out in the desert, or had it chosen him?* He shivered ever so slightly, and the world stood still for the briefest of moments. *Oh, Allah,* he thought, *was it really all WRITTEN?* just like Amira had told him that day when he had left her house to follow her instructions.

***

As Anwar stared at Amira's front door for the third time in his short life, he noticed that it was completely unchanged from when he had last seen it, but he also knew that *he most certainly had changed.*

Ten years ago he had been a young man, but now he felt weary and old, burdened by so many things he had tried to forget, and by so much pain and loss he had gone through. The decorative terracotta tiles around Amira's front door were still chipped and grimy. Anwar knocked and waited for the door to open.

Amira barely glanced at him when she appeared. Instead she turned her back on him and walked slowly into the same room he had found himself in ten long years ago. From somewhere to the side of the room Anwar could hear the anguished and deep voice of his father's favourite singer Umm Kulthum playing on the radio. *A sign* he wondered? *Was his father somehow directing him to be here?* Then, just as quickly as the thought had come to him, it disappeared and Anwar turned his attention to Amira.

She grasped one of his hands and led him to the middle of the old Persian carpet he had sat on ten years earlier, and it was only at that moment when she decided to look at him full on.

"Anwar, my boy, I have never forgotten you. My, my, you are

a man now, but a man with all the troubles of the world on his shoulders."

If Anwar was now so much older than his former self, then Amira too was undeniably older – a frail woman reaching the end of her days. Amira gestured for him to sit on the carpet and she did the same. Then, gently she took his left hand in hers and brushed his palm with her magical aromatic oil. She rubbed the oil into his hand with her thumb, closed her eyes, hummed as she usually did, then opened her eyes again and began to speak.

"Your life is about to change, my son. You have travelled a long and hard road, and you have been strong, but your heart is tired."

Anwar closed his eyes with relief. Amira had seen his dilemma; thankfully her powers were still intact. She continued to speak.

"You will meet a stranger near the pyramids and he will give you your treasure. Without this treasure you cannot go on."

"When?" Anwar demanded, suddenly grasping hold of the old woman's wrists with both of his hands in an unexpected act of violence.

"**WHEN YOU ARE READY!**" Amira replied, fixing Anwar with a steely glare. She was angry. He instantly withdrew his hands and lowered his gaze in shame; he had always respected the old.

"Am I ready?' he asked almost apologetically and with his eyes firmly fixed to the ground.

"Perhaps," said Amira, "but then again perhaps not. Your heart is ready, of that I have no doubt, but as for you – well I can't do your work for you."

Anwar bravely hid his disappointment; he had hoped for something a little more detailed from this old woman with the gift. Not only that, but this talk about his heart left him feeling confused and anxious. What did his heart have to do with anything which would help him in the future?

"Amira, will my heart speak to me?" he asked, almost pleading now for more information.

"As I have just told you my son, when you are ready – when you are ready. Now, I have given you all that you need to know so you must go. The future is waiting for you."

***

Amira slowly raised herself to her feet and then moved over to a large wooden table at the far end of the room. On it was a dish in the form of a scarab beetle; one of ancient Egypt's most sacred symbols. She dipped her thumb into the dish and gestured to Anwar to approach her. Anwar obeyed.

Gently, but firmly she took hold of one of his shoulders with her right hand, and looking up towards his face, but without making any eye contact, she used her other hand to press her oil-covered thumb hard between Anwar's jet black brows. It was only when she removed her thumb that their eyes met for the very last time.

Amira's eyes were piercing and otherworldly, and she repeated the same words to him as she had ten years earlier: "As Allah knows, it is written, my son, it is written."

THE DREAM

ANWAR walked out into the street and squinted as the bright sunlight hit his eyes. He was still angry and feeling desperate. Amira's words had given him no comfort whatsoever – instead they had disturbed him. He knew just how powerful her gift was, and how she had predicted the future for him ten years earlier when he had been so broken, but this time he hadn't wanted what she had given him.

None of what she had told him made any sense. He had been in the desert for so long now that he understood its language inside out. Strangers didn't just simply appear from nowhere, especially not a single stranger all alone, and nor for that matter at any of the pyramids he knew. Furthermore, all that business about his heart was still bothering him. *Why had Amira said that her prediction would only happen when his heart was ready?* As far as Anwar was concerned there was nothing wrong with his heart.

Yes, it was true that lately he was constantly consumed by a terrible and unpredictable fear, not understanding why it came and went as it did, but nothing the old woman had told him had any ring of truth for him.

Anwar glanced down the narrow alleyway and once again felt the oppressive feeling he always experienced when he was in Cairo. "This is not where I belong," he muttered to himself, and instinctively sensed that he needed to get as far away from the city as he could, and as quickly as possible.

After fifteen minutes he reached the stables where he had left his horse. The owner was still there playing backgammon with his son, and Anwar dropped the coins he owed him down onto the wooden board with his usual dismissive and contemptuous air. The owner looked up from the game and spat on the floor.

"Is that what you think of my stable foreigner? Well, don't come back, do you hear me? I have regular clients and I don't need your money."

"Hah, that's what your kind always says," Anwar replied mockingly, "but you'll take it anyway. You people of Cairo are all the same!" He then walked down the stable yard to where his horse was tethered and made sure that he didn't look back.

***

Although Anwar felt that his visit to Amira hadn't given him an answer to his fear, now that he was galloping free in the desert and miles from the city he was himself again. This was his true home. He didn't need people or their cities. That was a world that filled him with disgust and rage; a world which had given him ten years of despair and horror when he had lived with his uncle Mazir.

All he needed was this dry, clean air, the wind in his face and the occasional hawk in the infinite blue sky above him. As if in response to his thoughts a hawk suddenly appeared from nowhere and hovered high above him as he rode on. He felt the bird's power and freedom were exactly what he was experiencing at this very moment. The fear had left him and he was once more at peace and at one with his real world – the desert which had saved his life ten years ago.

After about four hours he finally arrived at his 'sacred place'. It was a chain of high dunes which overlooked three pyramids in the middle of the desert. This was part of a large area of territory that he and his men had captured years ago, and which had sealed his fate as the leader of their clan.

He dismounted from his horse and started to climb one of the dunes just as the sun was beginning to sink below the horizon. At the top he paused to take a deep breath. The climb had left him a little winded and he needed to allow himself to recover from the exertion.

He closed his eyes and listened as his breaths slowly became shallower and less frantic. Then he opened his eyes again to look out onto the pyramids in front of him.

These were no ordinary pyramids for Anwar. Although they weren't in any way as large as the Giza Pyramids, they had a magical and mysterious energy all of their own. When he came here, somehow he always sensed an indefinable peace and a healing of his burdens and troubles. Anwar was sure that it had been that energy which had triggered two astonishing dreams for him two years earlier.

Back then he had come to this dune after a particularly terrible battle against one of the worst clans in the southern desert. In fact, now that he thought about it, he remembered that the fear he felt inside himself had started just after that battle. He had lost two of his men, and almost lost his own life. His clan and he had won the battle, but only just, and the death of two of their comrades had shaken them all.

Anwar had noticed that after the battle his men no longer appeared to believe in him, and as the months had passed he began to sense that each man had decided to keep his distance from him because for them his power had gone. Kamal, his second-in-command, had been the worst amongst his cohorts for this. He was older than Anwar and for many years had borne a grudge against his chief for having been overlooked when the clan had decided on Anwar as their new leader.

Anwar had tried valiantly since then to reestablish himself with his men but had quickly realised that they had actively started to listen more to Kamal, and he had also seen how very often they would question and contradict his commands.

The consequences of this were inevitable. After nearly two years of unspoken insubordination from them, a week earlier they had just lost the latest of their battles, and with it a sizeable amount of territory. Three men had died, and the fear had returned to Anwar's heart with a vengeance.

***

Now, as Anwar stood at the top of the dune, he recalled that his two dreams of finding treasure in Andalusia two years earlier had come to him after he had decided on a final, desperate strategy in order to win back his 'comrades'.

One night Anwar had given them all a severe dressing down. He had then mounted his horse and ridden back out into the desert. He had calculated that perhaps a night without him would unsettle his men and make them realise that he was their one and only leader. Over the years he had learned that unpredictability was his best weapon in garnering his clan's loyalty.

That ride had taken him to this dune, and after looking out onto the pyramids as he usually did, he had laid down and fallen into a deep, deep sleep. It was in that sleep that he had experienced the strangest of dreams.

He had dreamed that he was back in Andalusia with his father and mother, but peculiarly this time they were not together. Instead Anwar was in the middle of a field and completely alone. Suddenly, an old Spanish shepherd appeared in front of him and poked him hard with his staff.

'You, stranger, get up," said the shepherd in Spanish, "I have a message for you".

He then began to tell Anwar that just beyond the next village, on the mountain road to Ronda, there was an old ruined church which stood high on a barren hill.

"You will find treasure inside that ruin; a treasure no one knows about. People have stopped believing in treasure, and so it has been there for more time than I can remember. Only a brave and honest boy will be worthy of finding it, and that boy will be you."

Anwar was stunned by the shepherd's words, and was just about to ask him who he was when the dream had suddenly ended.

On awaking, as he had begun to recall the details of the dream, and his mother and father, it was then that Anwar had started to cry uncontrollably. He hadn't cried like this since he had lived with his uncle Mazir, but now he could not stop the tears from falling. He missed both his parents so terribly. Neither of them had seen him grow into a man; neither had known about his life with his uncle and now this life in the desert with his clan.

And why, after all these years, when he had only ever dreamed about the umpteen battles he had fought, had he found himself back in Andalusia with his two most cherished loved ones – and yet not with them?

These intense emotions had made Anwar convulse with pain and he had curled his body into a small, foetal-like ball whilst he had continued to sob. After an hour he had felt completely drained of all energy and had instantly fallen asleep yet again, and once more he had found himself dreaming.

***

Again he was back in Andalusia, however on this occasion he

could see his father and mother were with him. They were all sitting on a bus and were on their way to Ronda for the annual fair. His father sat next to him whilst his mother sat a little way off talking to some local women in her perfect Spanish.

Anwar's father was telling him about his plans to spend a little more money this time and 'upgrade' their accommodation. There was a famous hotel in Ronda called La Reina Victoria, and Omar told his son that a very famous poet had once stayed there.

"Ronda is a place for poets Anwar," his father said. "We cannot dream the big dreams we once had, but when a great poet finds his dreams in a place like Ronda, then that is good enough for me." They continued to talk on the bus and Anwar told his father of his own silly, little rhymes.

"I make them up at school Father when we have our breaks. Sometimes I even sing them out loud to my friends. They call me the poet at school, but I didn't want to tell you because they are not real poems like yours."

His father laughed and ran his large, brown hand through his son's hair. "Ah, so now the truth is out!" he jested and planted an affectionate kiss on Anwar's cheek.

In the dream it was the end of the summer and still blisteringly hot. His father then began promising Anwar that they would camp under the stars as they always did each year.

"This time we'll camp in that old ruined church up on the hill overlooking the road." Omar told his son. "In Ronda I've heard a rumour that there is treasure buried inside that ruin. Everyone I have met says it is just a silly story from long ago, but maybe we will be the first to find it."

Anwar had been able to feel himself hugging his father tightly as the bus continued up the mountain road. His mother returned to her seat next to her husband and Omar shared the news with her that they would all be staying at the Hotel Reina Victoria as a special treat. Celeste clapped her hands in delight, kissed her husband and then drew her son close to her warm body.

But suddenly, out of nowhere, Anwar found himself noticing the old shepherd who had come to him in the first dream, and who had told him about the very same ruin up on the hill. His mother and father could not see the shepherd, but nevertheless he was there with them inside the bus. That was all he had remembered because moments after catching sight of the old man he had woken up.

PART III
REDEMPTION

THE DARKNESS BEFORE THE DAWN

ANWAR shivered and shook as he stared out again at the pyramids in front of him. Almost chilled to the bone, he seemed to have emerged from a trance-like state. As he returned to the real world, he remembered the prediction Amira had made many hours earlier.

He had only ridden out to his 'sacred place' to forget all of that, and had intended to stay for just a very short while because he knew that it was vital that he continued on his way back to the camp. But the pyramids had hypnotised him with their beauty and mystery, and he had found himself caught up in reliving those two incredible dreams he had experienced two years earlier.

His clan had not understood why he had said that he needed to go to Cairo that morning on urgent business. He had made excuses about having to see a family member. He knew that sharing the truth would have been far too dangerous; it was never an option for him. His men would have thought him weak and totally mad for consulting a fortune teller and besides, the fact was that his visit to Amira now felt like a world away.

She had talked all that rubbish about a stranger who would give him his treasure – *when his heart was ready* – and now standing in the dark and cold it all felt like a whole lot of idiotic mumbo jumbo to him; the fantasies of an old woman who no longer possessed her gift.

***

He had no idea how long he had been at the top of the dune.

All he knew for sure was that he had to return to his men as quickly as possible. Uncertainty was all well and good in small doses, but he had been away for far too long and there was a danger that they would begin to panic and think that he had abandoned them. His horse had wandered off from where he had left her hours before, and when he finally managed to reach her he mounted and rode like the wind back to the camp.

When Anwar arrived there was silence, except for the sound of his cohorts snoring inside their tents. The campfire had finally gone out, and as he walked over to his own tent to join his 'tribe' he caught sight of his second-in-command Kamal. It seemed that his 'comrade' had been waiting for him to return. Kamal turned to look at Anwar and then walked slowly over to him.

"So you're back," he snorted in disgust, "we thought that you had gone off to kill yourself. That battle was our worst. It must be still haunting you. Your honour and all that!"

Anwar could see that Kamal was beginning to consider himself the new leader now, and his fear returned to him in an instant.

"My honour is to lead my men Kamal!" Anwar retorted, his eyes piercing the eyes of the other man. "You are still learning what honour is my friend."

Kamal immediately sensed the threat in Anwar's words. He had seen Anwar be brutal with some of the men in the past. He knew what his leader was capable of, and so this was not the moment to attempt to defy him in any way.

Anwar noticed Kamal's hesitation and continued to call his bluff, even though the fear was still rising inside him.

"I know we have lost men and a large piece of territory, but we have not lost our presence in this desert. Most of the clans still fear us, and I have not finished with them yet. We will rise tomorrow, meet together and discuss our strategy and then we will mark our new territory a few miles south behind the pyramids. Now, go Kamal, you are wasting my time and yours."

The men separated without another word exchanged and returned to their tents.

***

In the morning Anwar could feel mutiny in the air. He had barely slept and was finding it hard to concentrate and speak to his men with his usual forcefulness and authority. Summoning all his strength, he told them of his plans for the new camp and how they would need to organise it.

He ordered them to spend the morning and afternoon checking every item of equipment, their water and food reserves, and also checking their stocks of ammunition. After that the only thing remaining would be to make sure that none of the horses was lame and then they would finally ride out to the pyramids.

Once there, they would turn south, and after two miles make camp. At this location Anwar calculated that the clan would only be eight miles from one of the desert's largest oases, and so would be able to renew their food supplies the following day.

When the time to set out came the light had already faded from the sky hours earlier. Anwar and his comrades mounted their horses and rode in a tight-knit group for about two hours until they reached the pyramids. They could see their dark silhouetted outlines in the moonlit night sky. Anwar brought his men to a halt and rode on ahead to show his men a sign of his leadership and power.

As he did so, he caught a glimpse of something at the top of the dune where he had fallen asleep and had his powerful dreams two years earlier. He drew closer and distinguished the outline of a human form. It was a boy, or a man perhaps; he wasn't quite sure. He signalled to his tribe to follow him.

This was something beyond an unusual occurrence. They were in the middle of the desert and no one was ever in this location alone. Anwar was familiar with mirages and strange images which jumped out of the desert when he was tired – he had experienced too many to count – so he was still not sure of what he thought he had seen.

He dismounted from his horse at the base of the pyramid and signalled to Kamal to do the same, along with all the other men. He informed them that he was afraid that there was a stranger in their midst. They followed him as he began to climb the side of the dune facing the pyramids. When they reached the summit, to their surprise they found nothing except for a large dark, round-like shadow.

The group approached it and saw that it was a hole. When they peered inside it there was momentary shock as they saw the dark human form of the stranger. This had been no illusion for Anwar. A small, thin figure sat crouched at the bottom of the hole and was scratching the ground with a rock.

**

"Hey, you," shouted Anwar, "who are you?"

The shepherd boy lifted his head in fright and saw the eyes of at least four men looking down on him. He could not speak.

"You, stranger," Anwar repeated, "who are you, who are you?"

"Salaam-Alaikum," (Peace Be Upon You) the boy cried out, his voice shaking with fear in an Arabic laced with a heavy Andalusian accent, "I am a friend, not an enemy." he added returning to his mother tongue of Spanish.

Anwar reacted in shock. *My God,* he thought to himself, *a boy speaking Spanish. What on earth is going on? This is mad, utterly mad!!!!*

"Ah, no entiendes amigo," (Ah, you don't understand friend) he shouted at the stranger in Spanish, "pues, sal de allí!" (Well, get out of there!)

The shepherd scrambled clumsily out of the hole he had been digging and cowered on the sand in front of these fierce-looking men.

"Who are you? What are you doing there?" Anwar barked.

"Don't hurt me," the boy whimpered, as if he were some kind of cornered animal about to be torn to shreds by a pack of wild dogs, "I'm not doing anything."

Kamal pulled the shepherd to his feet and slapped him hard across the face and then began to frisk him from head to foot, plunging his hands deep into his shirt and trouser pockets, but he found nothing. Noticing a pile of the stranger's belongings lying on the ground next to the hole, he grabbed hold of the pile and scattered the items onto the sand.

As he did so, he opened his mouth wide and gasped, stepping back in consternation as he saw what was lying on the ground. "Gold, Chief, gold!!!!!!!"

Anwar tried not to look as flabbergasted as his second-in-command, but he too could not believe what he was witnessing. A stranger at the top of this dune! A foreigner from Spain, and in possession of gold!

He snatched the ingot from the sand and gripped it tightly in his clenched fist.

"Well, well, well, just what we need!" he declared, spitting in the shepherd boy's direction. "He obviously found this in the hole and is trying to hide that fact from us. No man will ever leave his country and risk the desert for nothing."

Anwar turned to Kamal and threw the piece of gold at him.

"He is a liar this boy. He knows exactly where the rest of this gold is. Get him back in that hole, and keep him digging." Anwar's fear abated; he was once again in control.

Kamal grinned with a ferocity familiar to his leader, and pushed the shepherd straight back into the hole. The boy let out a cry of pain as he hit the bottom.

"Keep digging my friend," Kamal screeched in Arabic, and then turning to Anwar he asked, "how do I say that in his language?"

"Sigue," (Go on) Anwar shouted down into the hole, "sigue cavando tu pedazo de mierda!!!" (Go on digging you piece of shit!!!)

***

Hours later, as the dawn light began to break, the stranger crawled to the surface of the hole for the very last time and back to the men who sat waiting for his gold. He was covered in sand, his mouth and lips were dry and cracked from thirst, and his fingers were bleeding and lacerated. He had no gold in his hands.

Anwar felt the fear return to him. He had forced his clan to wait for hours at this dune whilst a strange, foreign boy had been digging for gold – and now there was none. He was failing again, and could feel that each of his men knew it. There was no way that he could allow this to go on; time was running out for him. Second by second he could sense that at this very moment they were coming close to concluding that he was not really the man he had led them to believe he was for so many years.

Kamal was already itching to become the clan's next leader and so, almost without needing to think, in an instant Anwar knew exactly what he needed to do in order to reestablish his authority.

"This stranger is not worth the skin he lives in." he shouted out to his men. "We'll show him what we do to people who waste our time like this."

Anwar pulled the boy towards him and looked deep into his blood-shot eyes.

"Scum that's what you are my friend. scum. No gold, no life!!!" and he turned to his men and ordered them to beat him.

The blows rained down on the boy, and his body started to collapse and fall into the dune. He felt a searing pain in his head as a blow hit him full on around his left eye. In an instant he suddenly understood that he was going to die. Panic rose inside his heart and he started to see images flash before his eyes.

The shepherd boy could see his father in his shop, his mother in her kitchen, and the village square in Andalusia where he had lived all his life. He suddenly saw the boat he had boarded to cross over to Tangiers, and the streets and alleys of that small Moroccan town. He saw the face of the girl he loved, and then heard the words of the man who had guided him on his journey. The boy remembered how the man had told him that money could never save a person from death.

In a flash he knew exactly what he needed to do. Nothing had ever been clearer to him in his whole life! He had to save himself from his own madness – nothing else mattered! Only his precious life and the precious lives of those he loved were of any importance.

"Stop, stop, stop, I'm looking for treasure." the stranger shouted out as loud as he could in his mother tongue. He had to survive. "I had a dream that I would find treasure near the pyramids of Egypt. Stop, please stop!!!"

**

Anwar could not believe his ears. Had he really heard what this foreigner had said? It was beyond ridiculous. In fact, everything that had happened since he had spotted the boy at the top of the dune had been utterly surreal. He held up his hand and shouted out a command to signal to his comrades that they needed to stop beating him.

"Have you just said that because of some idiotic dream, you have been digging this hole here to find treasure?" Anwar exclaimed in Spanish. He looked intensely at this stranger, realising that he despised him, and then began to laugh. His fear had disappeared completely. He gestured to Kamal to come over to where he stood.

"Leave him here," Anwar ordered, "you will never believe what he has just told me.' Kamal looked puzzled but Anwar decided to postpone his explanations until later. Confusion was another of his 'weapons' and had its own power; and power was exactly what he needed his men to see in him at this very moment.

Then, just as he was about to abandon the stranger Anwar seemed to change his mind. Instead he approached the boy and gripped the shepherd's neck tightly whilst still looking at his own men intently.

"You won't die my friend. I haven't done enough to kill you. A dream, eh, a dream? You have come all the way here just because of your crazy dream, and believe me scum, you will learn to regret it." And then he kicked the stranger as hard as he could. The shepherd howled in agony, his voice ringing out in the silence of the desert.

Anwar looked down on him once more and stabbed the ground next to the boy's face with his sword. "Dream on, foreigner dream on. That's all you have left!"

***

Turning away from the boy he signalled to the men that it was time for them to leave. He walked away and directed them to descend the dune from the same place where they had climbed up, but as they did so Anwar hesitated. There was something else he needed to tell the foreigner; something he had forgotten.

"Go on," he told them, "I'll be with you by the time you reach the ground; I've unfinished business with that little piece of scum."

He turned around and walked back to where the shepherd lay. The boy could barely raise his head but could clearly hear the last words which Anwar spat out to him in Spanish.

"Let me tell you, you little piece of vermin, you are not the only one who dreams. I had two dreams here two years ago at this very spot. In those dreams I was told that I would find treasure buried inside the ruins of an abandoned church in Andalusia, but I am not scum like you. I am a man who fights scum, and I would never be so crazy as to travel hundreds of miles just because of a dream!!!"

With that Anwar spat on the ground, and then stepping back from where the foreigner lay he suddenly noticed that Kamal had not descended with the others, but was standing close by waiting for him. Anwar returned to the limp body lying on the sand and kicked the stranger as hard as he could for the very last time and listened as more howls of pain filled the desert air.

"He's almost dead, but not quite." he shouted out to his second-in-command, knowing full well that Kamal would understand the message he was sending him. He saw his 'comrade' wince and smiled to himself. Slowly and deliberately Anwar walked towards him, knowing that at least for now he felt certain that he was still the leader of his clan.

But for how much longer? was a thought which unexpectedly entered his mind. This took Anwar completely by surprise and he stopped momentarily. His body shook and shuddered quite involuntarily and imperceptibly, and with that he felt the fear resurface inside him.

As far as omens were concerned, this was not what he needed right now.

TREASURE

THE next night, as usual, Anwar sat by the campfire with his cohorts, but this time he was more interested in watching his men rather than interacting with them.

His friends tossed the piece of gold they had found on the boy to one another and mocked this stranger they had met on the dune. These men had been Anwar's 'brothers-in-arms' for longer than he could remember, however tonight they seemed like childish adolescents. Not only that, but Anwar also knew that they were still extremely dangerous.

Even though he sensed that he had finally managed to convince them of his leadership when he had almost killed the stranger at the top of the dune, the fear inside him had returned. He knew that there would be other battles to come and some which these men would lose. Also, a few of them would die, and that fact alone made Anwar feel a deep sense of foreboding.

As these thoughts ran through his mind, he began to think about himself. Suddenly, and without any warning disgust welled up inside him rather than the usual bitterness he always felt. *Why had he been so cruel with the strange boy?* He knew that cruelty was often necessary with his men, *but why with this foreigner who had looked more like a boy than a man?* Also, he had spoken Spanish to him; the same Spanish he had spoken as a child when he had played with the other children in the streets of Tarifa so many years ago.

Anwar began to feel dizzy and nauseous, and his head started to hurt; he could not sit amongst his clan any longer. He made his excuses and retired to his tent. His eyes closed and again the dune appeared before him. He could not forget that they had found this stranger at the very place where he had experienced his two dreams of finding treasure buried inside the ruin of an abandoned church in the fields of Spain.

This was the ruin his father had mentioned in Anwar's second dream when he had promised his son that they would camp inside it under the stars and would perhaps be the first people to find that treasure.

The boy had also told him and his men about his own dream. He said that he had dreamed of finding treasure near the pyramids of Egypt. *A coincidence?* Anwar didn't believe in coincidences. His father had died at the age of twenty-nine and yet here Anwar was still alive at the very same age.

He rolled over onto his side, determined to fall asleep, but as he tossed around for hours on end, it became clear that sleep was not to be had – the skinny boy's words would not leave him.

***

As the last of Anwar's men found their own tents for the night, Anwar rose in the dark, mounted his horse and rode back to the dune overlooking the pyramids. Some force beyond himself had taken hold of him, and he knew that this almost 'supernatural' meeting with the stranger was bringing him to this place once again.

The dawn light was just breaking when he arrived at the hole where the clan had found the foreigner. Anwar suddenly felt foolish for having returned, yet also sensed that he was continuing to obey unseen commands which were compelling him to be here. The hole was still in shadow, but there was just enough light by which he could roughly see its depth. He jumped down into it and stood stock still.

Almost instantaneously a memory flashed into Anwar's mind. He was sitting at his father's market stall in Tangiers, and he could hear the words his father was saying to him.

"Anwar, son, life is not what we think it is. Look at that man over there. I don't know him at all. He is a stranger, but give a stranger bread Anwar, and you will never go hungry."

"…………..give a stranger bread Anwar." The words echoed in his mind. *Why now, after twenty years, did his father seem to be with him inside a hole overlooking the pyramids?* His heart was pierced by an unexpected and agonising pain. He and his cohorts hadn't given the strange, skinny boy bread; instead they had beaten him to within an inch of his life. And then Anwar had told him about his own ridiculous dream of a treasure buried in Spain.

Well, the boy had deserved it he reasoned with himself. *There had been something very irritating about him.* Anwar hadn't liked the fanatical expression on his face when he had grabbed hold of him and they had stared at each other for only the briefest of moments.

Perhaps it took one to know one was his next thought. Startled by this, Anwar began to feel his fear again. This time it was far more intense than before, welling up inside him and tightening its grip around his throat like some kind of invisible hand. And then seconds later he could feel it expand to the rest of his body, turning into paranoia. *What was happening to him? Was he going mad?*

***

As he stood in the hole, without understanding why, he

spontaneously found himself obeying instincts which he had long since learned to control. Prodding the ground under his feet with his sword, Anwar knelt down to see what he had unearthed. He pulled a piece of cloth from the end of the sword, and when he rose the dawn light revealed that it was a blood-stained shred of the foreigner's shirt. Anwar flung the cloth out of the hole in disgust.

He continued his prodding for a few more minutes, but the hole was just the same old hole he and his men had left behind the day before when the boy had confessed to his crazy dream. Anwar hauled himself out of this man-made tomb and gazed out at the pink light falling on the pyramids.

"Dreams, stupid dreams,' he cursed out loud to himself, "where are my dreams now? They left me the day my father died, that's what happened to them." Unlike the stranger, he wasn't so foolish as to believe in his own crazy dreams about finding treasure!

Aimlessly, Anwar found himself walking over to where the ragged cloth lay. He had tossed it further than he had imagined. Angry with himself for having returned to this place for what seemed like no good reason, he hooked the rag with the tip of his sword and flicked it away for a second time. To his shock and surprise he saw a scarab beetle lying on the sand where the cloth had been, and then suddenly the shepherd boy's words about his dream of finding treasure near the pyramids of Egypt flooded Anwar's mind once more.

He knew that in Egypt the scarab was a symbol of rebirth. He stared long and hard at its shiny shell and then, as if from nowhere, something unexpectedly opened inside him and a jumble of thoughts poured out.

So, was this why he had left his companions snoring in their tents? Was this why he had returned to the dune? Was this why suddenly, and with no warning, his father seemed to have come to be with him?

Was it time to become a man instead of the power-hungry person he had enjoyed being for so very long? Was that what the beetle was telling him?

Yet again Anwar became aware of the pain in his heart and he felt warm, salty tears slowly trickle down his cheeks.

***

"Damn," he muttered, "damn." He could not understand what was happening, but from somewhere deep within he knew that this moment was in some way sacred. Again Anwar's father's voice filled his head. He heard his laughter and felt his body close to his own. And with those sensations, suddenly great waves of fear engulfed him. *No, no, this wasn't happening to him. He had buried those memories long ago and had used all his willpower to forget the past.*

Anwar took his knife out of its sheath and cut deeply into his right forearm to rid himself of his father's voice and the feeling that he was just a breath away from him. It worked. Now all he could feel was the physical pain and the ribbons of blood trickling down to his wrist.

His gaze returned to the beetle which had not moved from its spot on the dune, and again that sensation of something opening inside him reappeared. Without feeling that he had any control over his actions, Anwar slowly inhaled deeply and placed the end of his sword into the golden sand. Then gently he traced a large circle around the spot where the beetle lay, and to complete the ritual, he stabbed the ground in the centre of the circle and straight through the scarab beetle's body.

Almost immediately Anwar's sword and almost half of his arm disappeared into the sand as it gave way under the force of his blow. Now on his knees instead of standing on the ground, Anwar found himself staring into a deep, cavernous hole in the dune. But unlike the hole he had just left, the bottom of this one was shiny.

The light blinding his eyes was not from the rising sun, but came from silver and gold. It shone from jewelled necklaces, crowns, rings, cups and vases all tangled together in a heap at the bottom of the hole.

No words came from Anwar's lips; not even his breath moistened the dry desert air. Time seemed to have completely vanished from the face of the earth. Only one sound filled the void both inside and outside his head; a voice he had once loved more than life itself.

"……………give a stranger bread Anwar, and you will never go hungry."

Anwar felt weakness overcome him and he let go of his sword, watching it fall into the hole as if in slow motion. The blood from his forearm wound continued to run down his arm and then he began to weep like a baby.

"Father, Father," he whispered, trembling as his words filled the empty desert air, "help me, please help me. I remember you, I remember you. I remember who I was – who I am! Help me Father, help me to remember. I love you, I love you, I LOVE YOU."

THE RETURN

WHEN Anwar finally rode into the camp later that morning, he found it almost deserted. Just three of his men had been left to guard it and the rest had obviously ridden to the nearest oasis in order to restock on food and water.

Farouk was the first of the men to spot Anwar and signalled to the others that their leader had returned. Anwar dismounted from his horse and untied the sack of treasure which he had slung across the horse's back. It fell noisily to the ground.

"What's that Chief?" Farouk asked, startled by the clanking sound. "It ain't a body, that's for sure. Sounds like you've found some ammunition!!!"

Anwar was in no mood to give any explanations to these men, and besides, what explanation could he possibly give? How could he tell them that he had returned to where they had left the stranger, and then by some miracle he had found the treasure they had all been hoping for in another hole on the same dune? No, that was not what he was going to say, either now or later.

He tried his best to ignore the men and walked in the direction of his own tent. Once inside he emptied the treasure out onto a large carpet which acted as a ground sheet and then sorted it into two large piles – one for himself and the other for his clan.

He knew that his men were not worthy of any of it, but then again, only a short while ago he too had been completely unworthy of this miracle. Anwar breathed in deeply and listened to his heart. It spoke only gentle words to him; words of comfort and compassion.

Finding himself with his father inside the stranger's hole had overwhelmed him. The pain of knowing that he really had been there, and yet Anwar had not been able to touch him or even bring him back to life, had been excruciating. However, now he also realised that all of this had been necessary. The pain had cracked open his heart, and his father's words had shaken him to his core.

If it hadn't been for his father's presence, and his words, and then the sight of the scarab beetle, Anwar would never have found his treasure.

Allah had been generous and merciful with him, and so it was only right that he should be generous with his men. He knew he was leaving them, and he also knew that this would change nothing for them. Kamal would take over as leader and they would go on to fight more battles. As Anwar projected his mind into the future, he understood that this life of wars and fights was no longer possible for him; his heart had turned away from it all the moment his father had come to him inside the hole.

He left half the treasure on the carpet and the rest he put back into the sack. He glanced around his tent which had been his home for ten long years and felt only relief that he no longer needed to stay.

***

Anwar walked out into the bright sunlight, and saw Farouk and the other men waiting for him. He approached them slowly, and then began to speak.

"I have further business to attend to in Cairo. It can't wait. I have left what you need in my tent. When Kamal returns with the other men, tell him that it is there."

The men looked at Anwar suspiciously, but sensed that it

was useless to ask any questions. Perhaps Kamal knew more about what was going on and would give them an explanation on his return. Anwar extended his hand towards the men, and shook each of their hands one by one. Then, not knowing exactly how to take his leave, he spat on the ground in his usual manner and simply turned around and walked back to where his horse was standing.

A few hours later he was once again at his 'sacred place' and standing at the top of the dune next to the hole where he had found the treasure. As he looked out onto his magical pyramids he began to pray for the very first time since his mother had died.

"Allah, I know not what I have done to deserve this salvation. I have been wicked in my life, but perhaps your love – and the love of my father and mother – have saved me."

No answer came in reply to Anwar's words, but the cold wind seemed to blow gently onto his face, caressing it just as his mother's hands once had only hours before she had died. As it did so, a memory suddenly flashed into Anwar's mind.

The stranger he had met at the top of the dune had been from Andalusia!!!

With that unexpected realisation, Anwar's mind shut down for an instant in utter amazement at what he had just been shown, and then after a second or two it re-awoke and a question surfaced abruptly without any warning. *Why hadn't he realised this at the time?*

Anwar had noticed the boy's strong Andalusian accent every time he had spoken, but had never thought anything of it. Then, as he continued to stand on the dune, staring out at the pyramids, another memory flashed into his mind – Amira's prediction.

Yes, the boy *was the stranger* she had told him about; the person she had said whom he would meet near the pyramids, and who would give him *his treasure!!!*

As Anwar began to process this memory, suddenly a second astonishing and totally unexpected realisation came to him. He now knew that none of what had happened on the dune had been an accident.

The stranger had given Anwar *his treasure* by telling him about his dream of finding it near the pyramids of Egypt, and Anwar could now see with utter clarity that he had done the very same thing for the boy. Unknowingly, he had given the stranger *his treasure* when he had told him about his dreams of finding treasure buried in an abandoned church in Andalusia!

For a second time, only nanoseconds after this extraordinary realisation, Anwar's mind momentarily shut down again, and when he finally returned to some kind of normal awareness he instantly understood that something far beyond anything words could ever reach had been given to him. A cosmic, invisible world had opened up before him.

It was a world that was ever present, but somehow only revealed itself in moments like this. Although he accepted that he couldn't see it, and nor could anyone else for that matter, nevertheless suddenly he realised that it was as real as the sand on which he stood!

***

Seconds after these epiphanies, Anwar suddenly felt himself in the grip of a deep understanding of what lay ahead of him;

he had had been shown his future. After around fifteen minutes of silent contemplation at the top of the dune, Anwar left his 'sacred place' knowing exactly where he would go. He needed to return to his grandparents' house in Cairo because now that he had his treasure he would try to persuade the new owners to sell it to him.

Two days later he was gazing up at the wooden shutters on the walls of the pink house which had once belonged to his grandparents. It had just been freshly painted and looked magnificent in the sharp noonday sun. Here Anwar was, only for the second time in his life, in front of this house which had once been his home. The day before he had learned that the house was for sale. *How in God's name did these things happen?* he wondered.

It was incredible to be feeling so different on this pristine winter's day from the man he had been only a few days ago. It was almost as if he had been reborn. Like a butterfly he had escaped his chrysalis and was now embarking on a new life, far from what he had lived in the desert. Anwar walked up to the front door of the house and stared long and hard at the same bell his mother had rung twenty years earlier when they had first arrived from Tangiers.

He knew that he was finally ready to return to the world; a world he had abandoned ten years before. The future – his future which had been revealed to him as he had stared at the pyramids – was now so very obvious to him. He would live here in his old home and begin to write poems which would change people's lives; just as his father had always dreamed of doing.

He would find time to visit Amira again to let her know that she had been right: he *had* met a stranger near the pyramids because *his heart had been ready.* And that stranger *had given him his treasure!* He would even share some of it with Amira;

that was the least he could do for the old woman with the gift.

He would also take a ship from Alexandria to Marseille to see if he could locate his mother's brother and sister. They had been much older than Anwar's mother, and so had stayed behind when Celeste and her brother Mazir had left France for Egypt with their parents.

And finally, he would return to Tangiers to find Ahmed's family, and then journey on to Andalusia and Ronda to stay in The Reina Victoria Hotel. Perhaps he might even find love there in that town made for poets!

***

Yes, all of this he would do in order to honour his past and also bring love to those around him. But, before any of those dreams could be fulfilled, Anwar also knew that his heart was asking him to do something of immense and immeasurable importance; something which could not wait.

It would be necessary for him to confess and tell his story to others so that they would understand all the terrible mistakes he had made, and why. Only the truth told from a deeply contrite heart would rid the world of its cruelty, violence and menace. Amira would be so proud of him!

Anwar sensed that not only had *his* time come but also the time *for the whole world.* It was time for this world to become a place of peace: a place for poets, painters, writers, singers, and all kinds of dreamers. A place in which everyone would be able to turn away from their own darkness and heal their broken hearts – no matter how long it took. That was what he wanted more than anything else.

Anwar breathed in deeply and pressed the bell next to the door of his grandparents' house and waited in nervous anticipation. Even though he was completely sure of what he was about to do, he knew that he still didn't quite understand how he had found the courage to return to Cairo and his old home. This was the city that he had hated with such a passion, along with its inhabitants, and where he had endured so much suffering.

But in the last few days everything, yes EVERYTHING had changed, and he was now finding himself praying with all his might that he would be able to live here once again!

Thirty seconds passed and he began to sweat and shake a little. Anwar tried desperately to visualise the pyramids he had looked out onto two days earlier; he needed their strength and magic now more than ever. A few seconds later the door swung open and he saw the agent who had agreed to show him the house.

"Ah, good day Sir," the man said in a rather formal, yet friendly manner, "so you managed to find us! Please come in. I don't think you'll see a better home in the whole of Cairo. Bigger ones, of course, but nothing like this. It's an utter gem."

Anwar was about to answer the man but then decided to keep quiet; some things were sacred and better not shared at certain moments. He entered the familiar, dimly lit hall and suddenly found himself gripped by a strong wave of grief. He could see that the mosaics and frescoes he had known in his childhood were still decorating the walls.

"Yes, I see what you mean." he finally answered, hoping to be able to disguise his pain, and then with that he followed the agent down the long corridor. At the end was an open doorway leading to a brightly lit room which Anwar remembered was the kitchen. He had spent so many hours there with his grandmother, watching her cook and prepare the family meals.

He followed the agent in and to his utter astonishment saw

a woman leaning over the stove, and a man standing next to her. On hearing the visitors, the woman turned around and Anwar nearly fainted. He could not believe what he was seeing! Those eyes, nose and mouth were so familiar to him. It was his mother!!!

She began walking towards him, smiling and opening her arms wide to greet him. She was young again, and full of life. Anwar stood completely frozen to the spot for a second or two, once again unable to take in what he was witnessing. He blinked several times, but the vision remained and he began to shake uncontrollably.

"Welcome home, my son, welcome home; we were waiting for you!" he heard his mother cry out, and behind her he saw the man. He had moved forward too, and was smiling the widest and brightest of smiles Anwar had ever seen. His young, handsome face was full of joy; a joy that filled the whole room with a soft, yet vibrant light. It was his father!!!

***

Anwar could hear the sound of music in the background, and recognised the voice of his father's favourite singer: Umm Kulthum. And then suddenly, he heard another voice he knew so well. It was coming from inside his head, and he could just about distinguish the faint rasp of the old woman. It was Amira. She was saying something to him, something very familiar, but this time there was only sweetness and love in her voice.

"As I told you my son, Allah knows everything; it is written, it is written."

FINAL NOTE

SO, you see dear friend, life is far stranger than we can ever predict. This has been the imagined life and journey of The Alchemist's *other hero*. With it the truth has been told and Paulo's iconic story – loved by millions – is now complete.

Above all, the spiritual message of The Alchemist is a transcendental one. It wants to show us that the heart of life is paradoxical, and that we can only find our light when we are willing to face our own darkness. This was what Santiago experienced when he clung onto his dream of a treasure he so desperately wanted to find in a hole in a dune, until the spectre of death finally loosened his grip. Only then, in that moment when death stared him brutally in the face, was he able to surrender and thus receive his treasure.

This 21st Century we are now living in is showing us my friend just exactly how much darkness remains inside our hearts and souls, and so Anwar's story as well as Santiago's are more relevant today than ever before. We continue to fight wars, pollute and destroy our planet, and want to have as much as we can, and as soon as we can by using others and our planet's resources for our own selfish, egotistical ends.

But, in the final analysis, as Santiago discovered in The Alchemist, his treasure was his own precious life – and by extension the lives of those he loved – and then Anwar too discovered that life is really all about love; the love we can share and give to one another. These are discoveries we are all destined to make in our own lives because we come to Mother Earth in order to specifically redeem the darkness within ourselves.

I know that for many people this is something that they are

not really aware of, but it explains the reason why Paulo Coelho's fable became such a publishing phenomenon. The Alchemist had quite unintentionally hit a subconscious transcendental 'nerve' in each of us – our spiritual hunger for a love beyond our egos. A love we call Divine.

Anwar's father was able to show his son the way out of his darkness through his love for him. That love was demonstrated in many ways, but was also symbolised by the instruction Omar gave to the young Anwar in his childhood:

"……..give a stranger bread Anwar, and you will never go hungry."

This symbolic bread we give to a stranger must be the way forward for every one of us, and surprisingly the stranger I talk about in my fable is not just outside ourselves, but also within us. All too often we try to 'kill' our inner selves just as much as when we go about trying to metaphorically 'kill' others outside ourselves. Anwar spent so much of his life doing just that before his own unexpected redemption.

We know from all the violent conflicts we witness around the world, and the pain and alienation we experience on a daily basis, as well as all the health issues we face, what NOT SHARING AND CARING for our inner strangers and the strangers outside us has done to ourselves and to our world.

As so many activists remind us with such urgency,
we are quite literally becoming extinct,
along with our beloved Mother Earth.

If my fable can do one thing and one thing only, as it reveals the truth of what the famous story by Paulo Coelho is really all about, then I hope it can galvanise us all into understanding that our fears, hatred, wounds, defence mechanisms and selfishness twist and defile our hearts and souls and destroy any chance for a new beginning.

I know that the default position for us as human beings is to refuse to believe that there is so much darkness within each of us, and this denial is an intrinsic part of our human condition as spirits living a *material life* on Planet Earth. However, when we scratch the surface of ourselves we discover that there is a sizeable amount of cruelty inside all of us, and also that each of us is, my friend, to a lesser or greater extent broken-hearted.

But I have enormous faith in Mankind, and also compassion for every one of us, including myself, and hope that we can all look upon each other with that compassion. If we do, I am sure that we can then begin to make the changes needed to save ourselves from the worst of ourselves, and also save this beautiful planet we know as HOME.

Despite geeky fantasies of being able to live on Mars and build houses on the moon in the very near future, the truth is that there is no other *physical home* for us than the one on which we live.

OUR TREASURE, DEAR FRIEND,
IS CLOSER THAN WE THINK.

ABOUT THE AUTHOR

KAREN Williams was born in London in 1958 to a Russian mother and English father. Karen believes that we are all born into our destinies, and hers knocked on her door at a very early age.

Whilst Karen's classmates played games, she worried about the state of the world. As she grew up, this young misfit tried her best to adapt to societal expectations, but after completing a degree in psychology, as soon as those studies were over, her REAL LIFE began. The confusions, questions and pain which hadn't found answers in conventional life became the driving forces of her life.

Those questions led Karen to Andalusia, southern Spain in 1984, and ten years later cosmic forces of fate met their young pilgrim when she embarked on an extraordinary metaphysical journey. That destiny was to be the living out of Paulo Coelho's fable THE ALCHEMIST – a story which had psychically predicted the trajectory of her own life.

From 1995 till 2014 Karen threw herself into an incredible spiritual quest, in which she dared to step out of all conventional parameters and follow her inner light. Her spirit was in search of itself – her inner TREASURE – and that search almost cost Karen her life. The toll on her health was huge, but despite the suffering she endured, it allowed her to demonstrate that we all carry the light of truth within us. It is the Light of Divine Love.

Society may wish to rob us of that truth, and no more so than with the lies and propaganda which emanate from people like the current President of the U.S. with his catchphrase 'Fake News'. Nevertheless, if we are prepared to stake our lives on what we know deep inside our hearts and souls, we will be the winners in the end.

Karen continues to follow a mystical path to this day. Her main goal is to be as loving a person as she can, and to never let her inner darkness get the better of her. Karen's passions are studying the After Life through Near Death Testimonies and also championing environmental issues in any way the universe sees fit. All of this means listening to the inner promptings of her intuition, regardless of whether or not her life makes any sense to the outside world.

You can find Karen on her Facebook page: **Treasure: A Soul Journey With The Invisible.** You can also read about her quest in **TREASURE: A Soul Journey With The Invisible. NEW EDITION III.** Available on Amazon.com and other online book sellers.

Printed in Great Britain
by Amazon